To Mr. Toad

This book belongs to:

Published by Ladybird Books Ltd
27 Wrights Lane London W8 5TZ
A Penguin Company
3 5 7 9 10 8 6 4 2

First published by Ladybird Books Ltd MCMXCVI   This edition MCMXCVII
LADYBIRD and the device of a Ladybird are trademarks of Ladybird Books Ltd

© Colin and Valerie King MCMXCVI
The author/artist have asserted their moral rights

In comes
the tide

Colin and Valerie King

Ladybird

In comes the tide, over slimy green rocks.

Out goes the tide, washing everyone's socks.

In comes the tide, bringing billowing sails.

Out goes the tide, taking sea-spouting whales.

In comes the tide, splashing pirates of old.

Out goes the tide, leaving cargoes of gold.

In comes the tide, with sea horses prancing.

Out goes the tide, crusty lobsters are dancing.

In comes the tide, bringing Neptune the King.

Out goes the tide, leaving jellies that sting.

In comes the tide, with gigantic white waves.

Out goes the tide, over shipwrecks and caves.

In comes the tide, on a bright, moonlit night.

Out goes the tide, it's a smuggler's delight.

In comes the tide, see the octopus wobbling.

Out goes the tide, leaving walruses squabbling.

 In comes the tide, the Admiral has landed.

Out goes the tide, all his shipmates are stranded.

 In comes the tide, to islands of sun.

Out goes the tide, while monkeys have fun.

 In comes the tide, bringing fishermen home.

Out goes the tide, rolling seals in the foam.

 In comes the tide, with a thunderous roar.

Out goes the tide, to some other shore.